W9-BWL-552

SPARKY THE SPECTACLE
LORNA THE LAZY
ANDY THE ARROGANT
SELMA THE SPOILED

MEGHAN THE MUTE
GREER THE GREEDY
GILLIS THE GLUTTONOUS

THE Quickerwonkers
PAPA THE PROUD
MAMMA THE MEAN
GILLIGAN THE GUIL

EVANGELINE LILLY is an actress who first broke to fame through her role as fugitive-on-the-run, Kate Austen, in JJ Abram's hit television series, LOST. She took a respite from acting after completing shooting the film Real Steel (2010) to focus on her family life and her foremost passion: writing.

While filming The Hobbit Trilogy with Peter Jackson in New Zealand (2012) Evangeline met Johnny Fraser-Allen and together they began work on the book that you have in your hands: The Squickerwonkers.

This is Evangeline's first published work and she is honored to share it with you.

You can visit her at: **www.evangelinelilly.com**

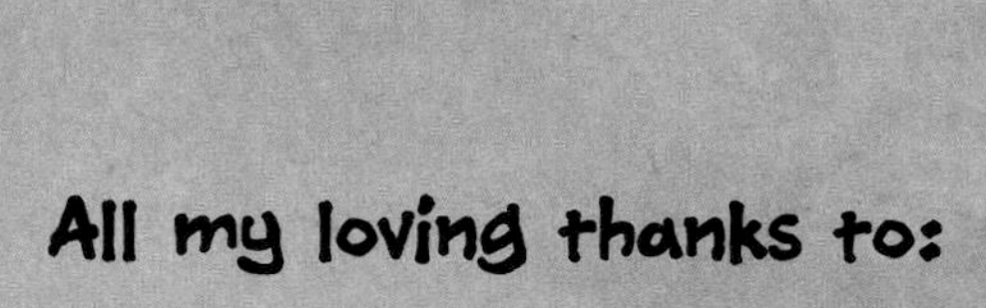

All my loving thanks to:

Johnny Fraser-Allen, my family,
Richard Taylor, Martin Baynton,
Jess Cole, Sam Maydew,
Stephen Lambert, Tane Upjohn-Beatson,
Fran Walsh, Philippa Boyens,
Peter Jackson, Greer Townshend,
the friendly folk at WETA workshop,
Laura Price, Nick Landau, Tim Whale, and
Chris McLane at Titan Books and mostly
to Norman and Kahekili.

I couldn't have done it without you.

JOHNNY FRASER★ALLEN is a senior sculptor and conceptual designer at WETA Workshop where he has worked since his teens. His film credits include Andrew Adamson's Narnia Chronicles, Stephen Spielberg's Tintin, and Peter Jackson's King Kong and The Hobbit Trilogy.

Johnny is currently working on a series of illustrated Young Adult novels titled The Gloaming Trilogy: **www.thegloamingtrilogy.com** You can follow The Gloaming Trilogy on facebook for book release updates and current exhibition dates.

Special Thanks to: Jim Henson who taught me of Dragons, for my mum and pop who carried me to their eyries, and for Richard Taylor who taught me how to fly them, thank you.

Special mention to Tania Rodger and Guillermo Del Toro for believing in me and nurturing my work, and a big thank you to Max Patté, Rob Baldwin, Amy Fitzgerald, Joy Buckle, Mary Pike, Tristan McCallum, Emma Bartlett, Katherine Tuttle, Tiger Von Stormborn and especially Nick and Claire Laing, could not have got this far without any of you.

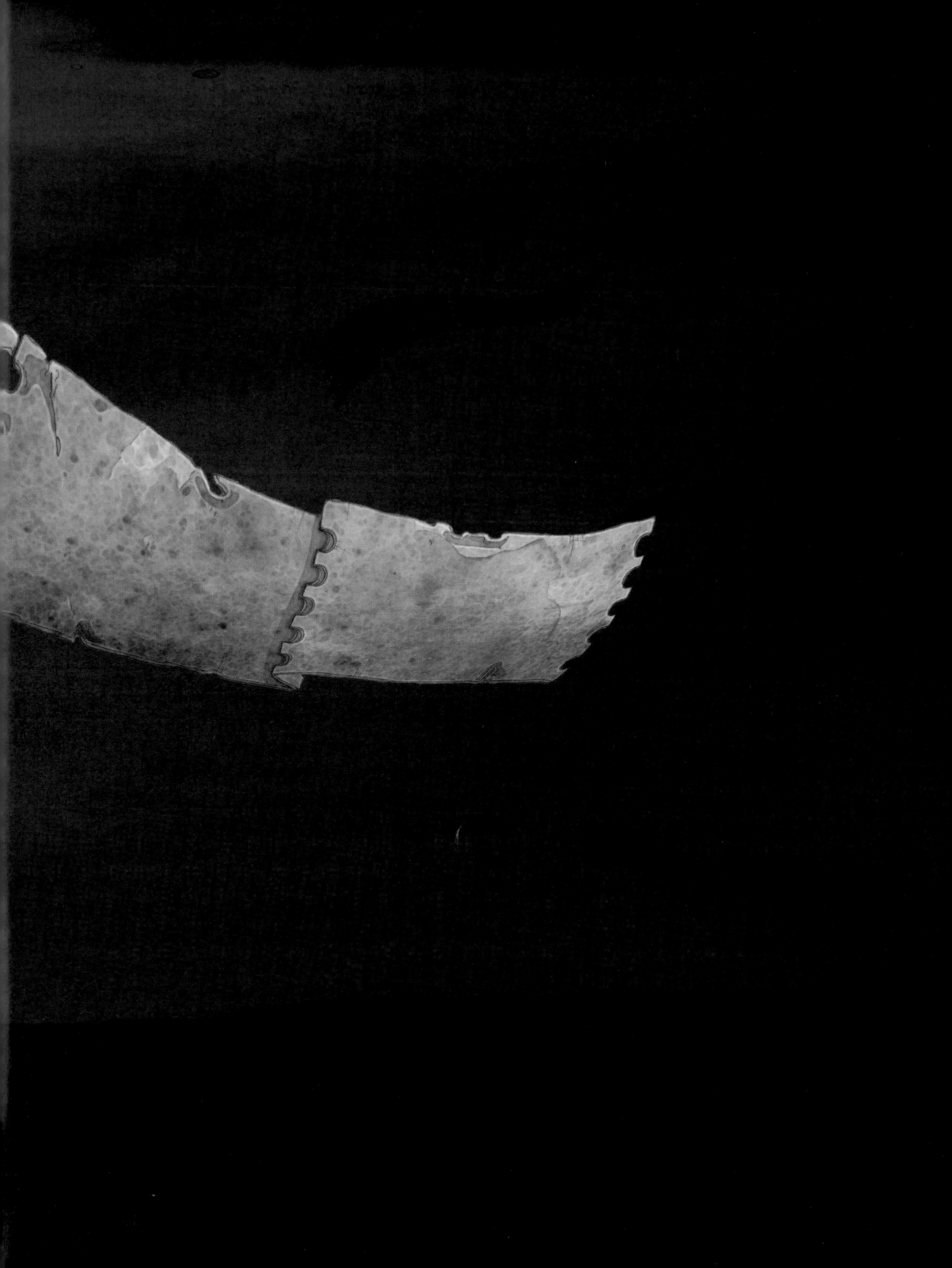

And so the girl learned, on that rueful night,
Not to be too quick to judge,
There's a devil inside,
She might like to hide,
...But what if one gave it a nudge?

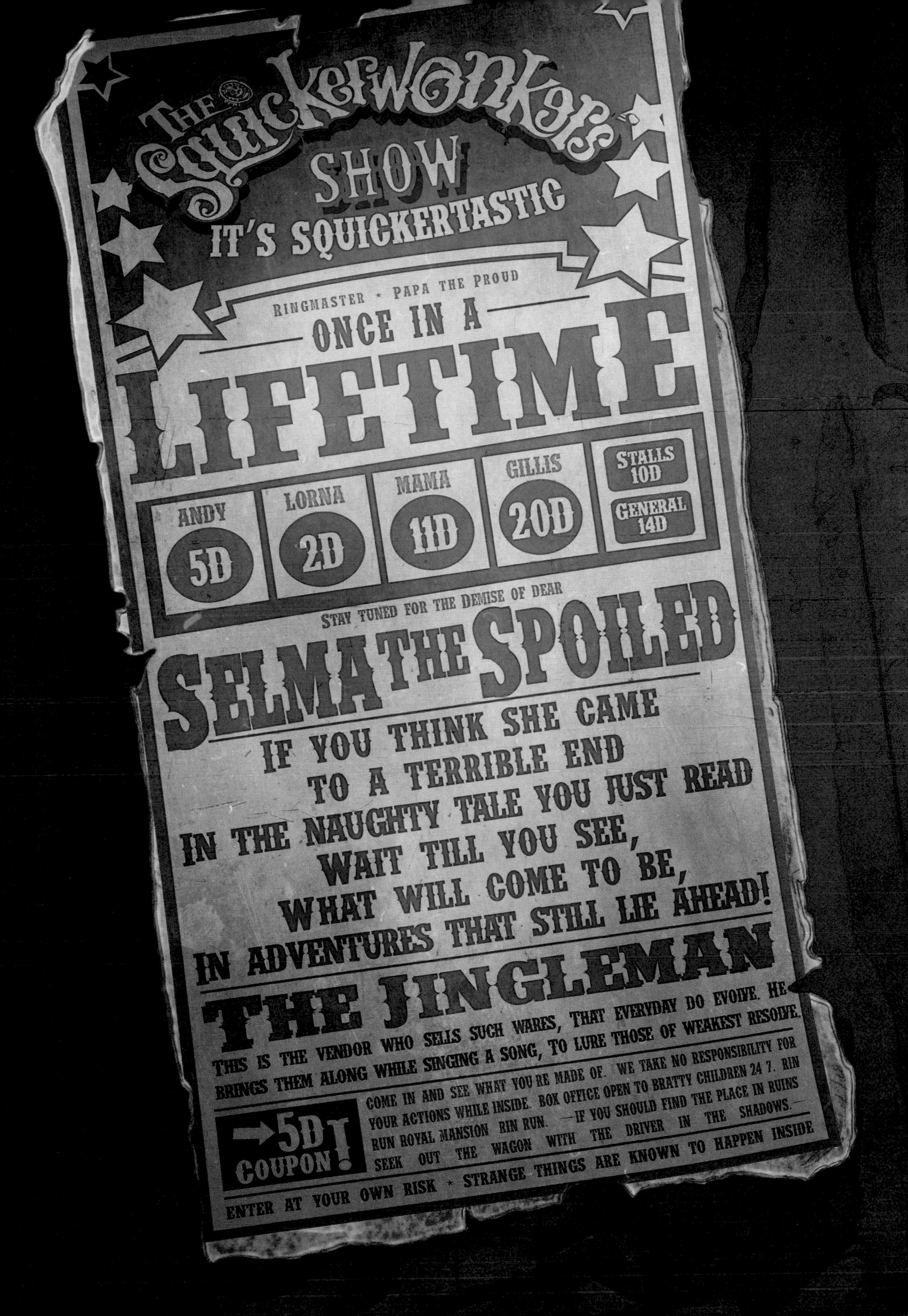

THE Squickerwonkers SHOW
IT'S SQUICKERTASTIC
RINGMASTER ★ PAPA THE PROUD
ONCE IN A
LIFETIME
ANDY 5D
LORNA 2D
MAMA 11D
GILLIS 20D
STALLS 10D
GENERAL 14D
STAY TUNED FOR THE DEMISE OF DEAR
SELMA THE SPOILED
IF YOU THINK SHE CAME
TO A TERRIBLE END
IN THE NAUGHTY TALE YOU JUST READ
WAIT TILL YOU SEE,
WHAT WILL COME TO BE,
IN ADVENTURES THAT STILL LIE AHEAD!
THE JINGLEMAN
THIS IS THE VENDOR WHO SELLS SUCH WARES, THAT EVERYDAY DO EVOLVE. HE
BRINGS THEM ALONG WHILE SINGING A SONG, TO LURE THOSE OF WEAKEST RESOLVE.
5D COUPON!
COME IN AND SEE WHAT YOU'RE MADE OF. WE TAKE NO RESPONSIBILITY FOR
YOUR ACTIONS WHILE INSIDE. BOX OFFICE OPEN TO BRATTY CHILDREN 24 7. RIN
RUN ROYAL MANSION RIN RUN. —IF YOU SHOULD FIND THE PLACE IN RUINS
SEEK OUT THE WAGON WITH THE DRIVER IN THE SHADOWS.—
ENTER AT YOUR OWN RISK ★ STRANGE THINGS ARE KNOWN TO HAPPEN INSIDE

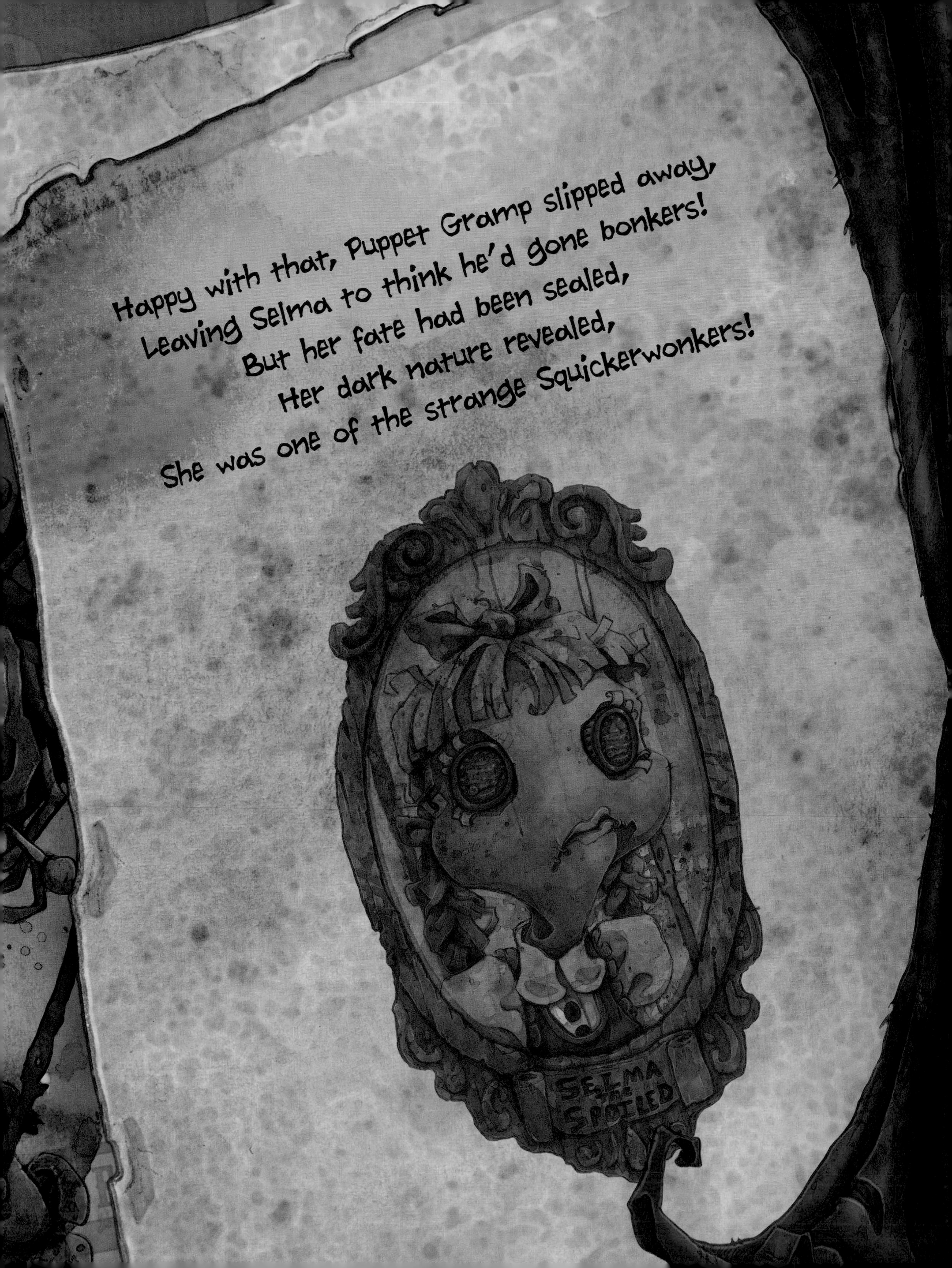
Happy with that, Puppet Gramp slipped away,
Leaving Selma to think he'd gone bonkers!
But her fate had been sealed,
Her dark nature revealed,
She was one of the strange Squickerwonkers!
SELMA THE SPOILED

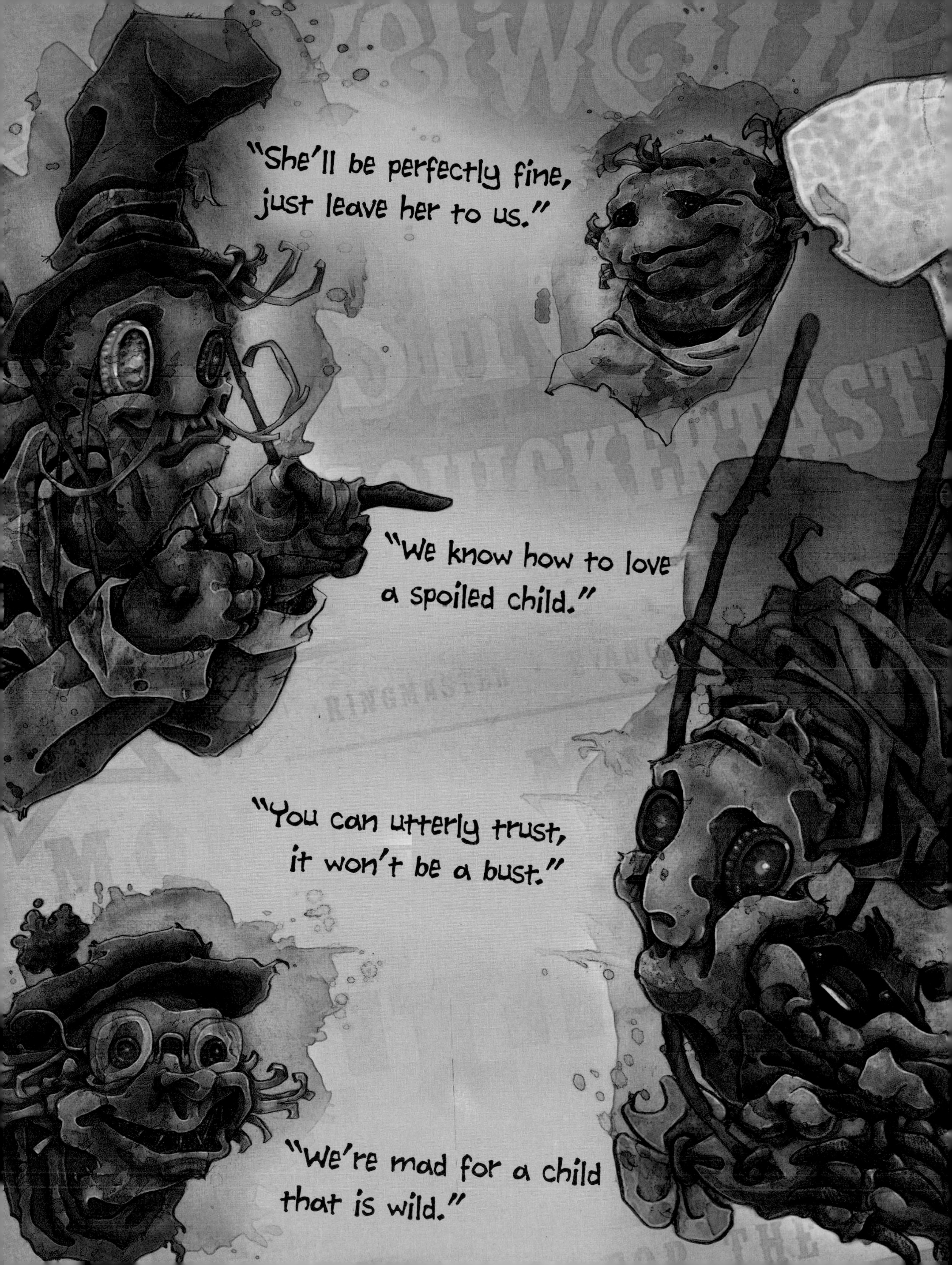
"She'll be perfectly fine,
just leave her to us."
"We know how to love
a spoiled child."
"You can utterly trust,
it won't be a bust."
"We're mad for a child
that is wild."

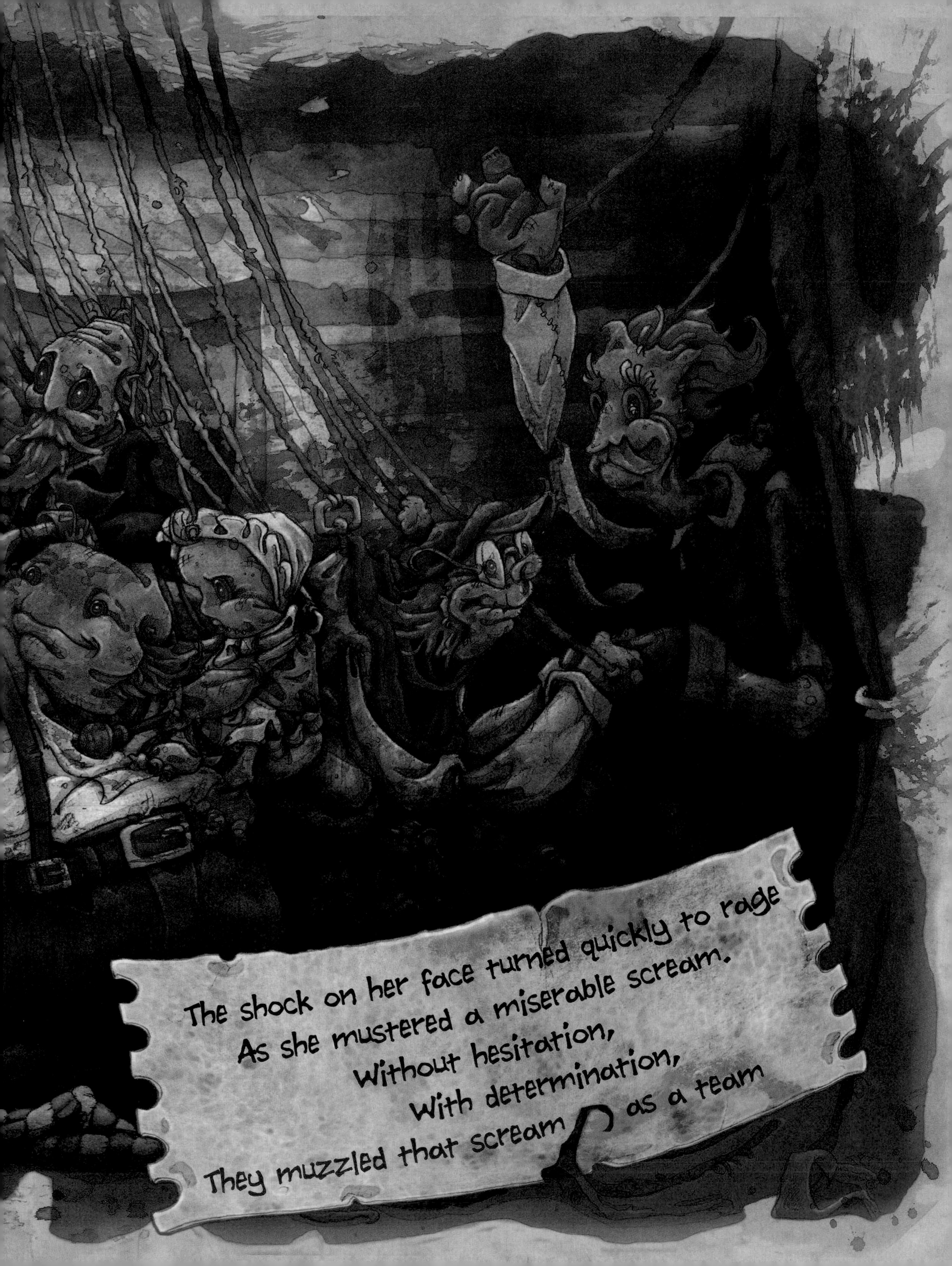
The shock on her face turned quickly to rage
As she mustered a miserable scream.
Without hesitation,
With determination,
They muzzled that scream as a team

"If you take this girl into your
group,
And love her as if she's your own,
If you give her your care,
I'll make you the heirs
Of the Rin-Run family throne."

With those choice words,
a change did take place
Taking Selma the Spoiled by surprise.
Her strings were attached,
Her clothes became patched
And she suddenly
had coins for eyes!

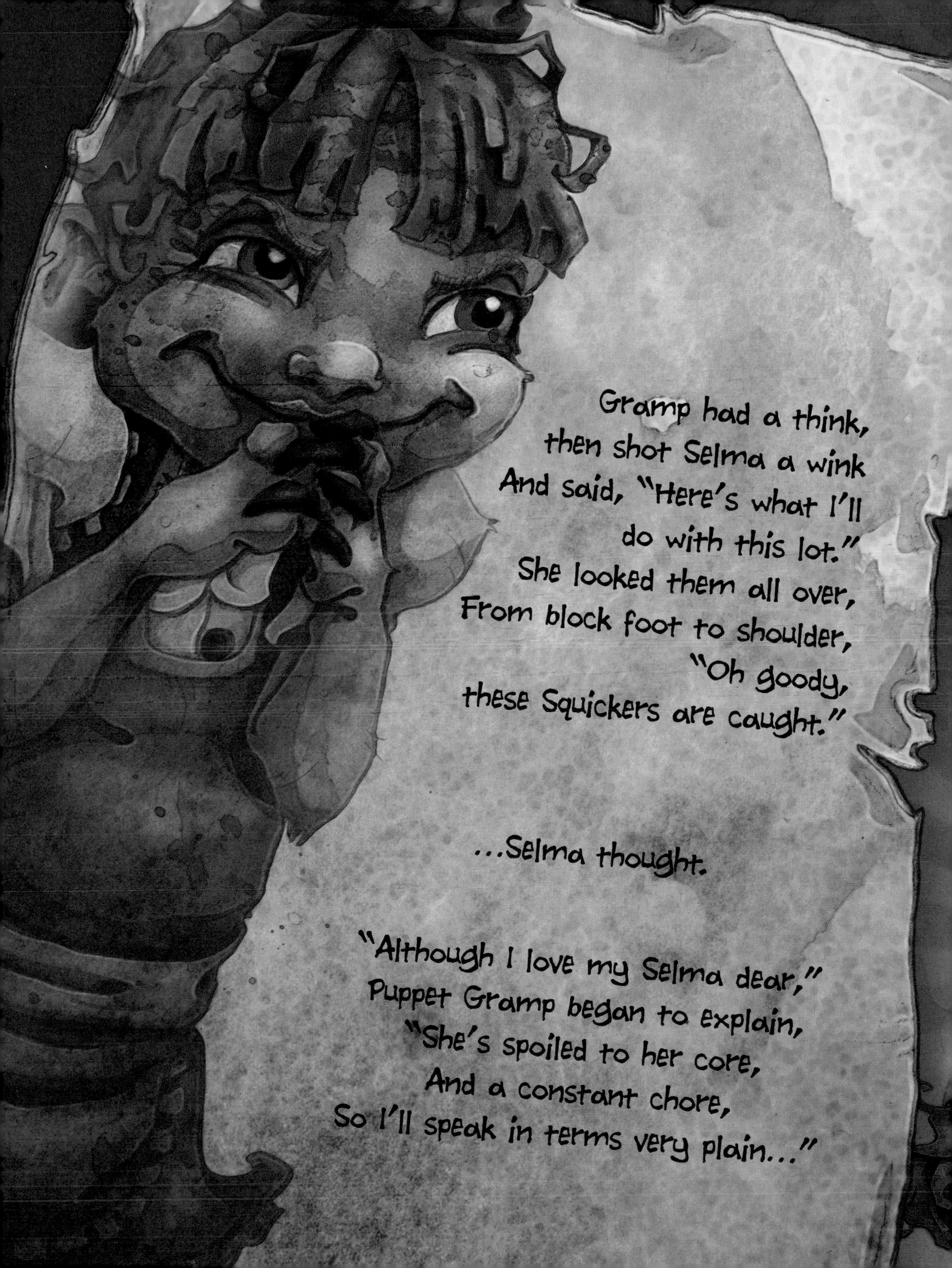

Gramp had a think,
then shot Selma a wink
And said, "Here's what I'll
do with this lot."
She looked them all over,
From block foot to shoulder,
"Oh goody,
these Squickers are caught."

...Selma thought.

"Although I love my Selma dear,"
Puppet Gramp began to explain,
"She's spoiled to her core,
And a constant chore,
So I'll speak in terms very plain..."

"They popped my beautiful red balloon,
And for this you must have their heads!"
The Squickers drew near
And with voices sincere,
Begged her, "Won't you show mercy instead?"

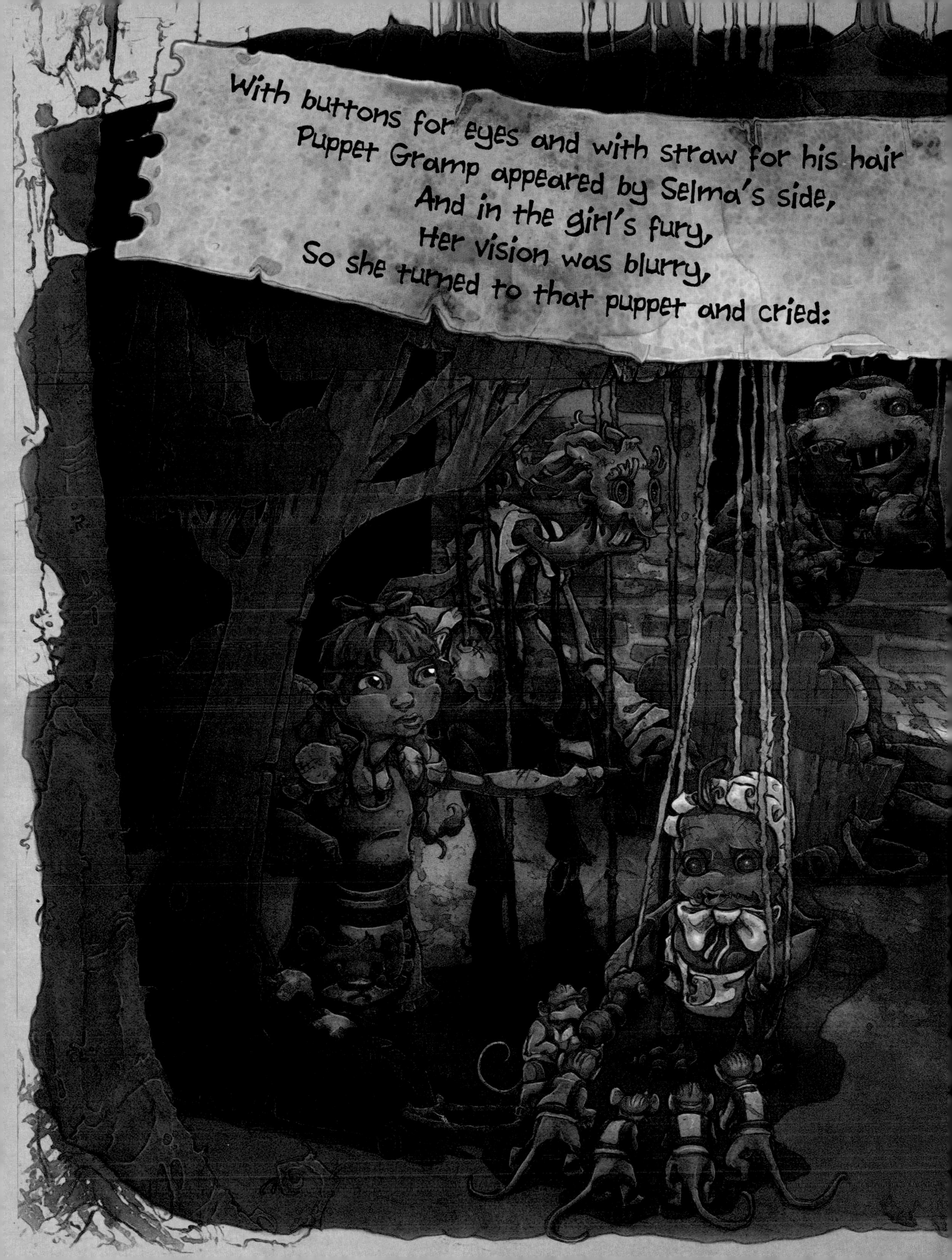
With buttons for eyes and with straw for his hair
Puppet Gramp appeared by Selma's side,
And in the girl's fury,
Her vision was blurry,
So she turned to that puppet and cried:

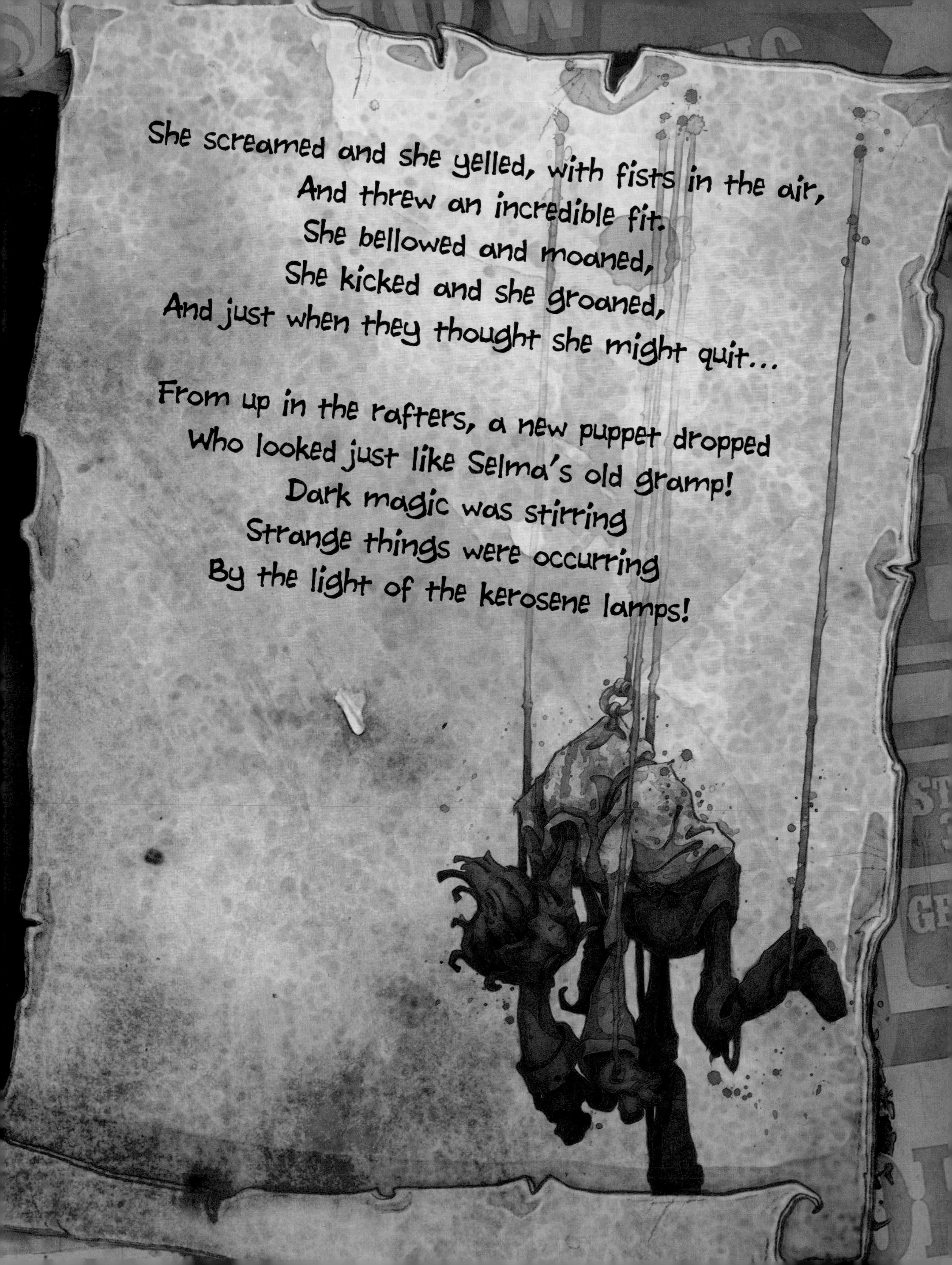

She screamed and she yelled, with fists in the air,
And threw an incredible fit.
She bellowed and moaned,
She kicked and she groaned,
And just when they thought she might quit...

From up in the rafters, a new puppet dropped
Who looked just like Selma's old gramp!
Dark magic was stirring
Strange things were occurring
By the light of the kerosene lamps!

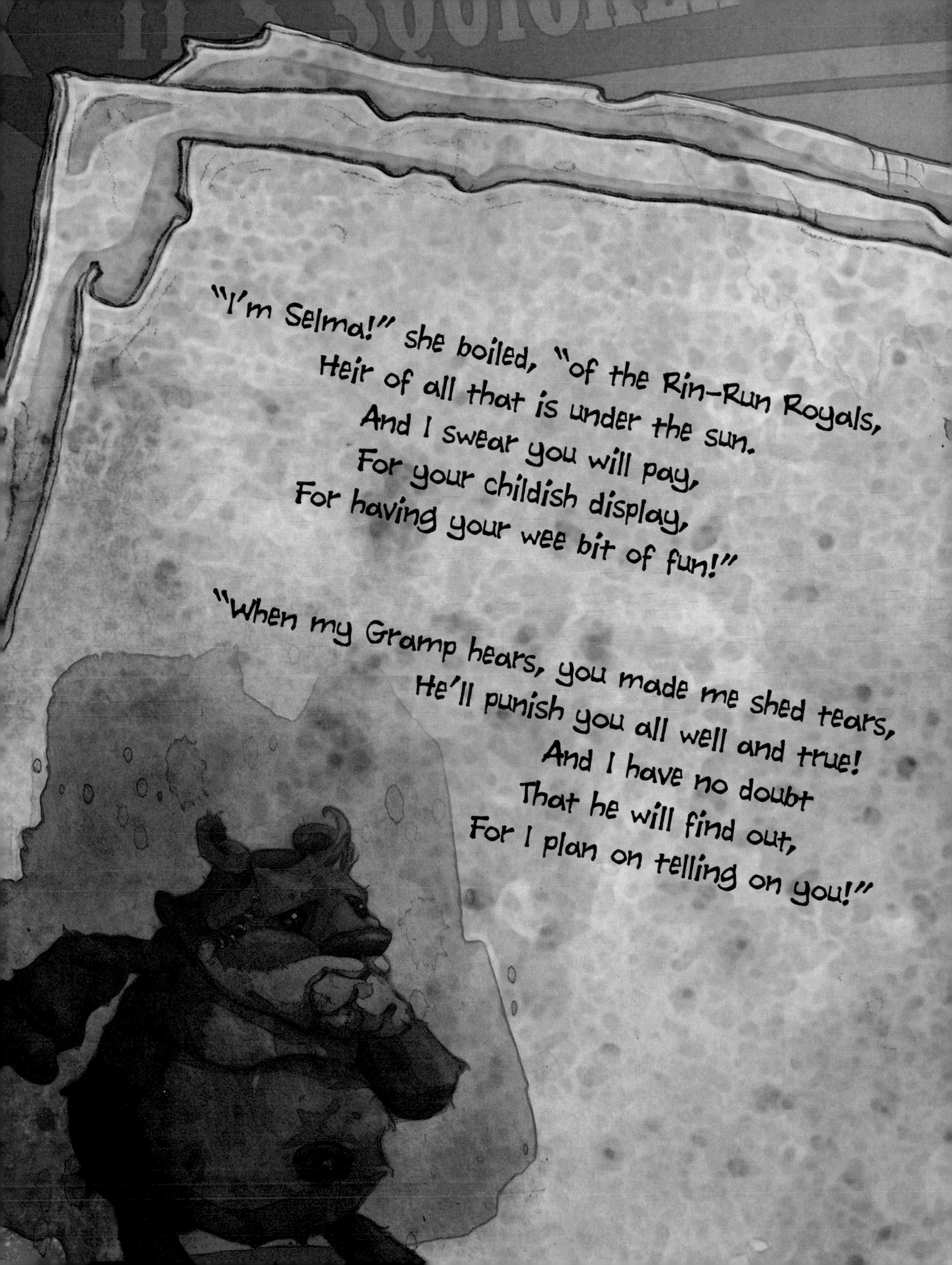

"I'm Selma!" she boiled, "of the Rin-Run Royals,
Heir of all that is under the sun.
And I swear you will pay,
For your childish display,
For having your wee bit of fun!"

"When my Gramp hears, you made me shed tears,
He'll punish you all well and true!
And I have no doubt
That he will find out,
For I plan on telling on you!"

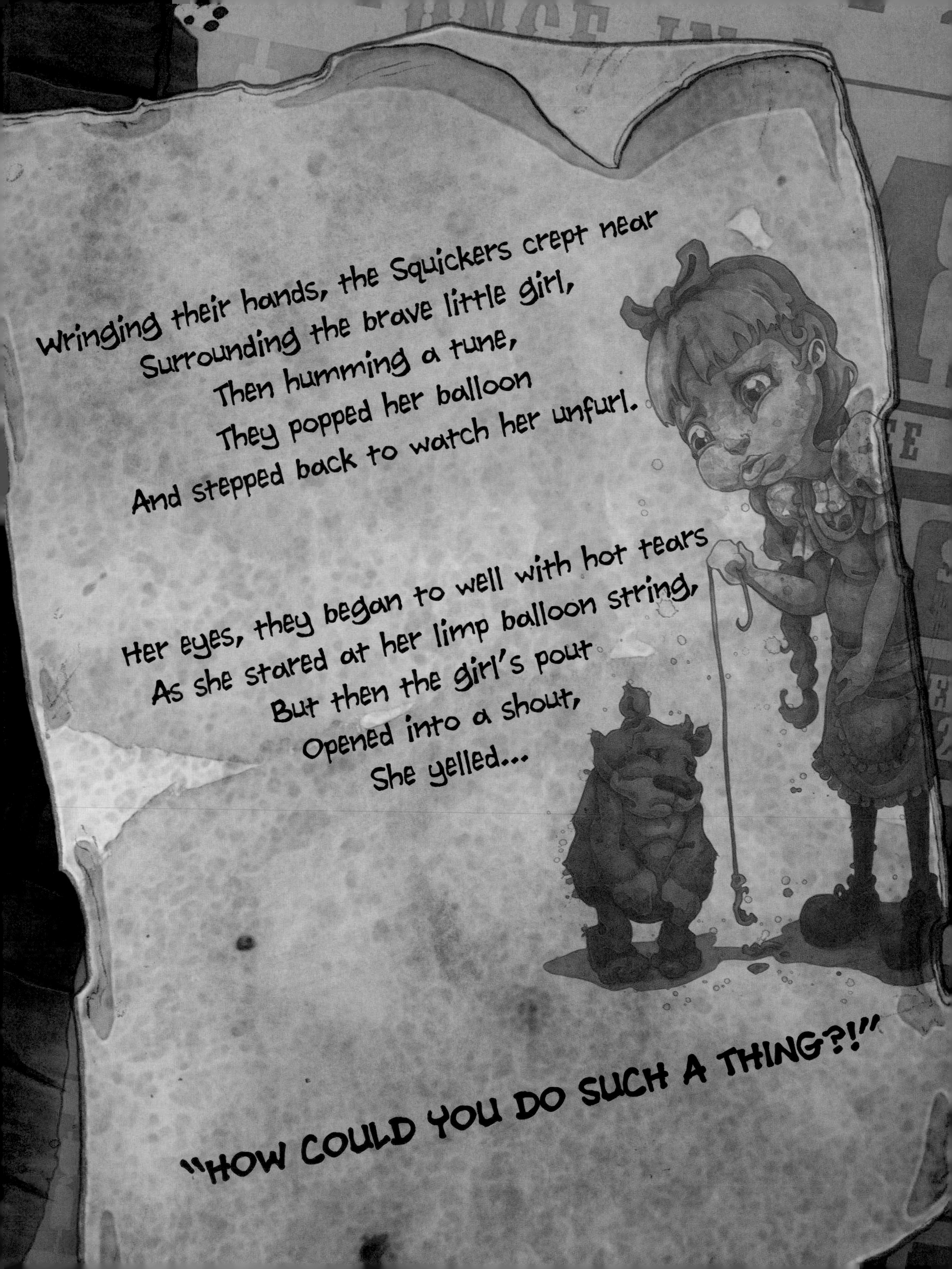
Wringing their hands, the Squickers crept near
Surrounding the brave little girl,
Then humming a tune,
They popped her balloon
And stepped back to watch her unfurl.
Her eyes, they began to well with hot tears
As she stared at her limp balloon string,
But then the girl's pout
Opened into a shout,
She yelled...
"HOW COULD YOU DO SUCH A THING?!"

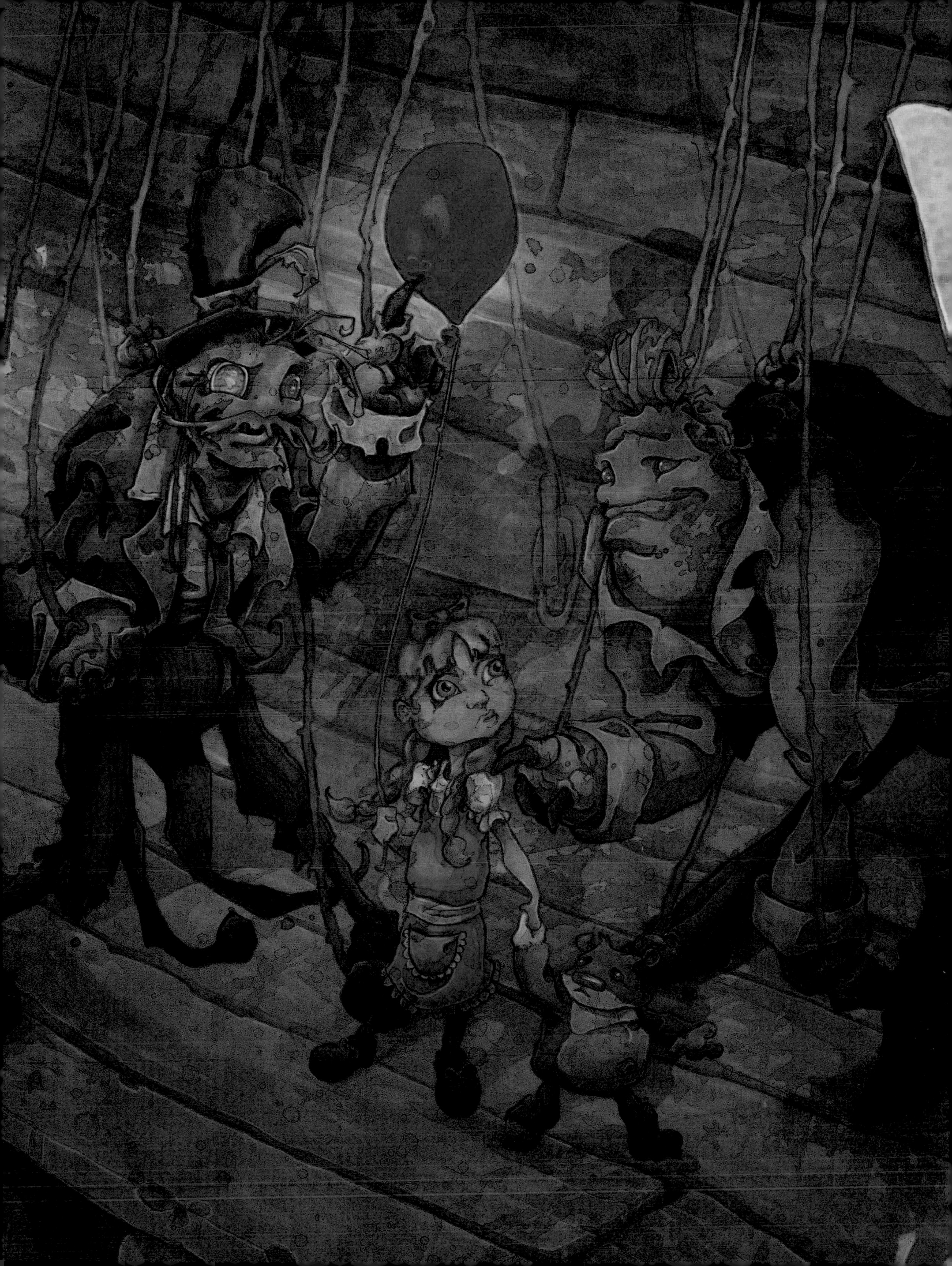

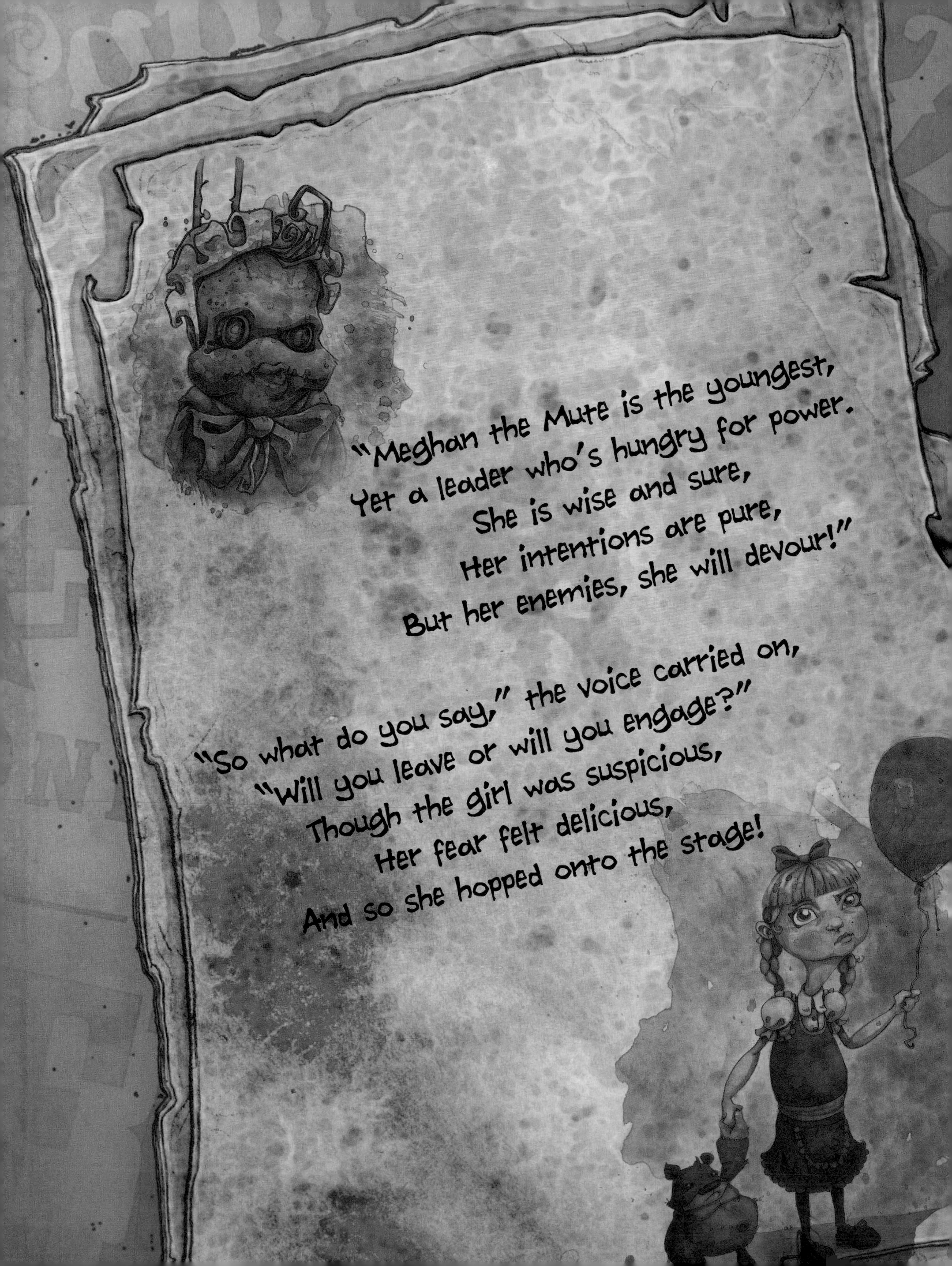

"Meghan the Mute is the youngest,
Yet a leader who's hungry for power.
She is wise and sure,
Her intentions are pure,
But her enemies, she will devour!"

"So what do you say," the voice carried on,
"Will you leave or will you engage?"
Though the girl was suspicious,
Her fear felt delicious,
And so she hopped onto the stage!

Meghan the Mute.

"Gillis the Gluttonous has a heart of gold,
But a body of doughnuts and pie.
He does all his eating
As if he's competing,
And sadly he's painfully shy."

"Beside him is Sparky the Spectacle,
The ham of our curious brood.
He likes to tell jokes,
Loves ladies and smokes,
And to our dismay, he's quite crude."

Gillis the Gluttonous
and
the Spectacle

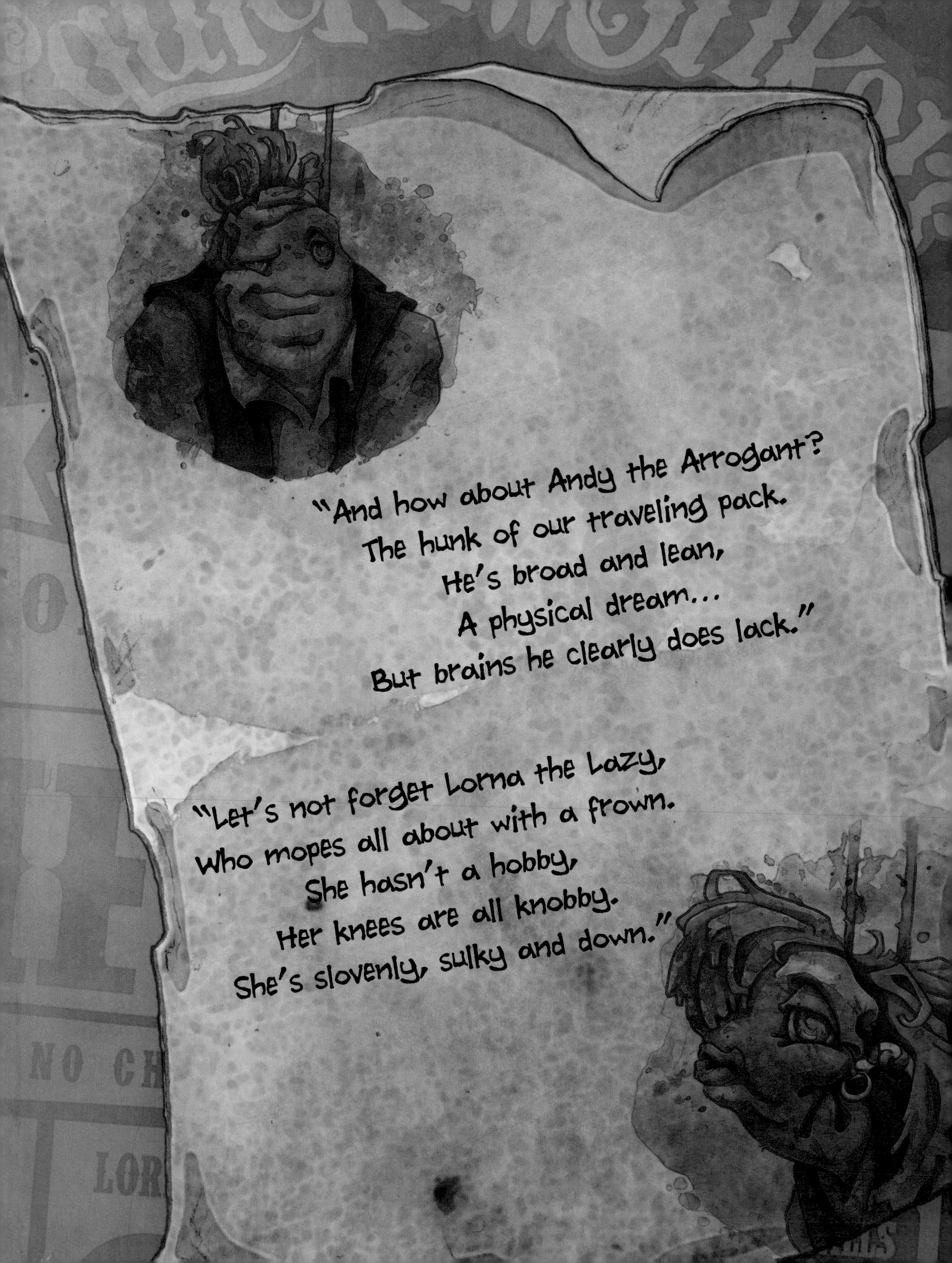
"And how about Andy the Arrogant?
The hunk of our traveling pack.
He's broad and lean,
A physical dream...
But brains he clearly does lack."
"Let's not forget Lorna the Lazy,
Who mopes all about with a frown.
She hasn't a hobby,
Her knees are all knobby.
She's slovenly, sulky and down."

Andy the Arrogant
and
the Lazy

"Then there is Gilligan the Guilty
Who frets and worries all day,
Following his wife,
the love of his life,
Who takes but never does pay."

"Her name is Greer the Greedy
A thief with a great sense of flair,
She loves to pick pockets,
Small purses and lockets
And hide what she finds in her hair."

Greer the Greedy and Gilligan the Guilty

Papa the Proud
and
Mama the Mean

"The head of the Squickerwonker troop
Is known as Papa the Proud.
He has terrible airs,
Never mingles or shares
With commoners out in the crowd."
"The colossal woman on his arm,
The crowd calls Mama the Mean.
Just follow the trail,
Of what is derailed,
And that is where Mama has been."

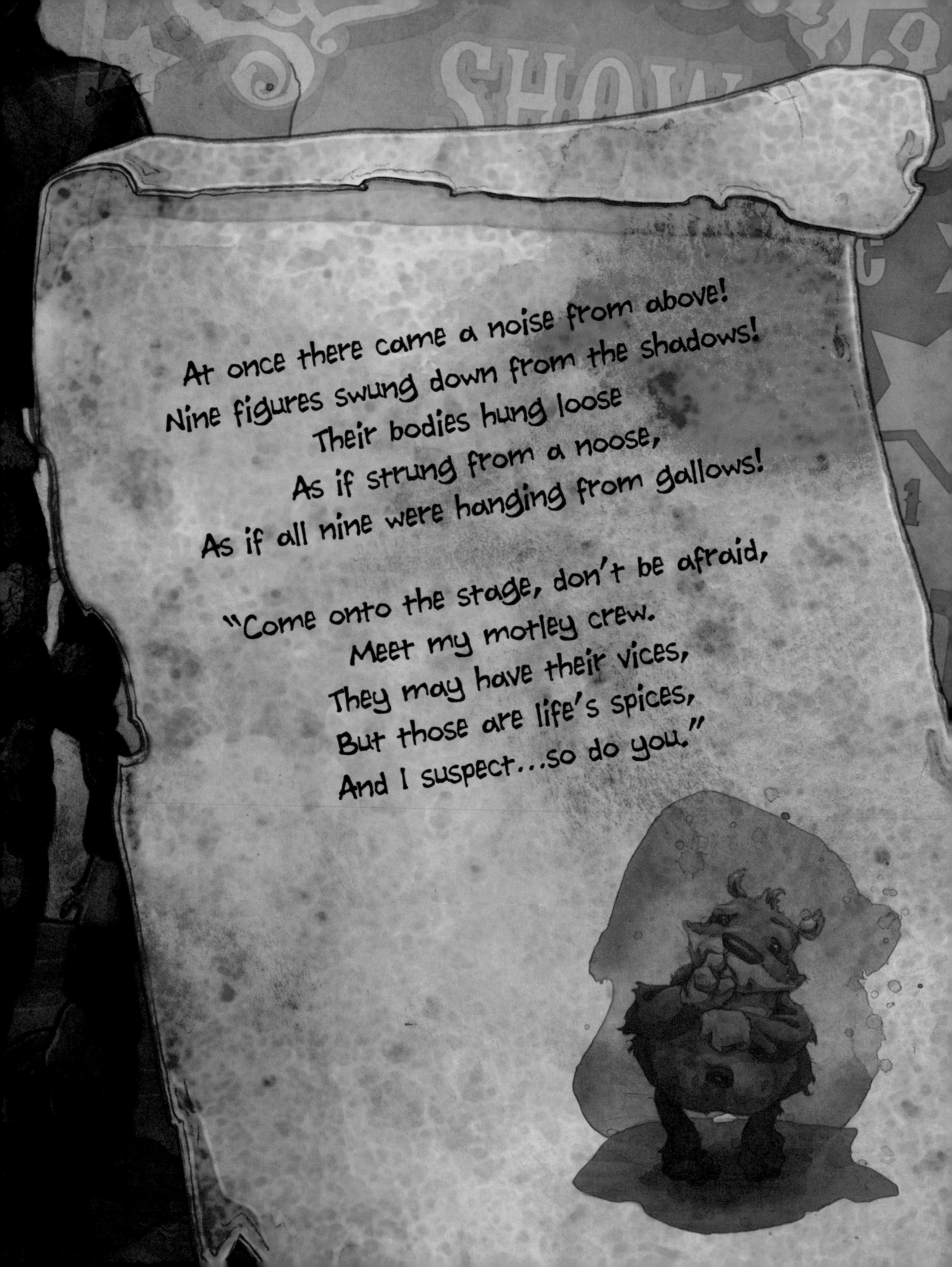

At once there came a noise from above!
Nine figures swung down from the shadows!
Their bodies hung loose
As if strung from a noose,
As if all nine were hanging from gallows!

"Come onto the stage, don't be afraid,
Meet my motley crew.
They may have their vices,
But those are life's spices,
And I suspect...so do you."

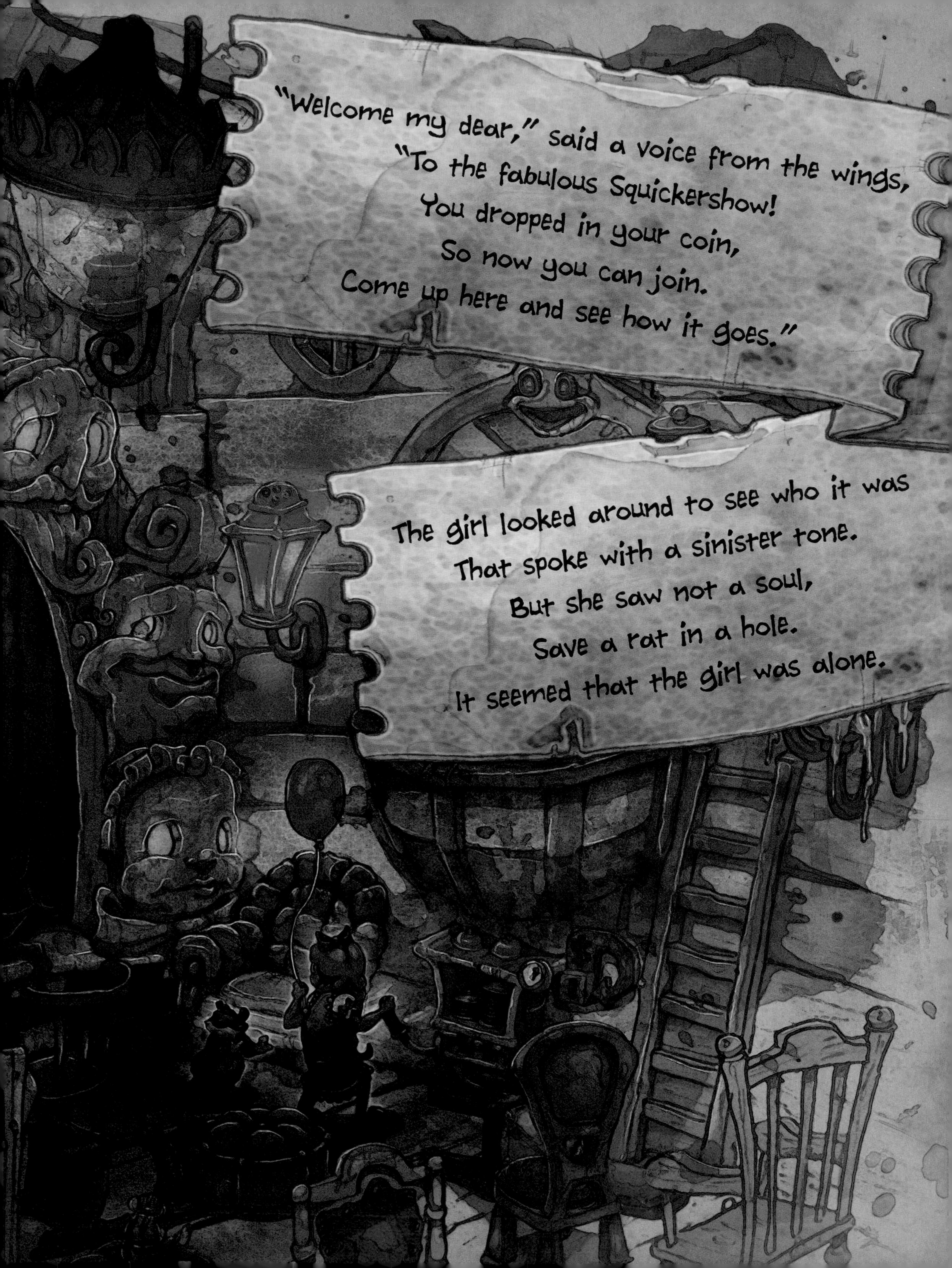
"Welcome my dear," said a voice from the wings,
"To the fabulous Squickershow!
You dropped in your coin,
So now you can join.
Come up here and see how it goes."
The girl looked around to see who it was
That spoke with a sinister tone.
But she saw not a soul,
Save a rat in a hole.
It seemed that the girl was alone.

THE

Evangeline Lilly
Illustrated by Johnny Fraser-Allen

The Squickerwonkers
ISBN: 9781783295456

Published by Titan Books
A division of Titan Publishing Group Ltd.
144 Southwark St.
London
SE1 0UP

www.evangelinelilly.com
Silver Lining Entertainment
421 S. Beverly Dr
7th Floor
Beverly Hills, CA 90212

Book design by Stephen Lambert and Evangeline Lilly.
The text for this book is set in Ashcan BB

First Titan edition: November 2014

A CIP catalogue record for this title is available from the British Library

10 9 8 7 6 5 4 3 2 1

Printed in The USA

There once was a clever and passionate girl
Who wandered away from a fair.
She ventured inside
A wagon-like ride,
And what did she find in there?

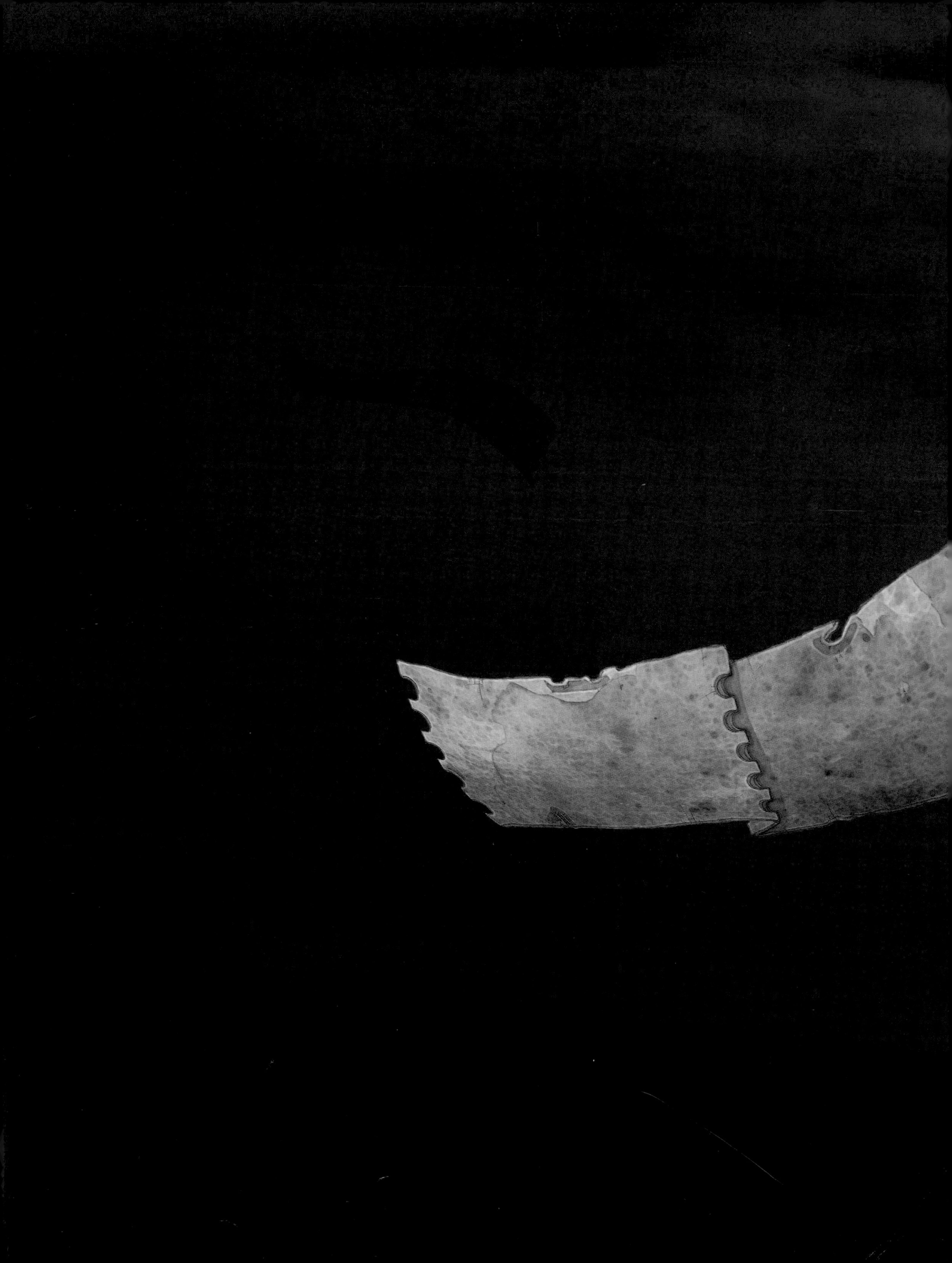

FOREWORD

by Peter Jackson, Fran Walsh & Philippa Boyens.

Every now and then, if you are lucky, you come across a story full of magic that feels as if it has always been there, sitting somewhere out on the edge of imagination just waiting to be discovered.

The Squickerwonkers is just such a wonderful tale. Cleverly told and stunningly visual, children of all ages will delight in the book's deliciously dark mischief. The playful rhyme beckons the reader in, inviting them to look closer, for in this book, nothing is as it seems. It was a joy to watch this curious cast of characters dance across the page. Selma of the Rin-Run Royals is indeed a young lady to be reckoned with.

Evangeline Lilly and Johnny Fraser Allen have created something remarkable - a truly original story. We can't wait to see where the Squickerwonkers take us next!

I dedicate this book to my mother,
who's believed in this story since she first read
it... twenty years ago.

-EL

I dedicate this book to my
Goddaughter, Freya Leonie Laing.

-JFA